READ with me! *has been written using about 800 words and these include the 300 Key Words.*

In the first six books, all words introduced occur again in the following book to provide vital repetition in the early stages. The number of new words increases as the child gains confidence and progresses through the stories. After Book 6, a wider range of vocabulary is used but each word is repeated at least three times within that story.

The stories centre on the everyday lives of Kate, Tom, Sam the dog, Mum, Dad, friends, neighbours and relations. This setting often provides a springboard into Tom and Kate's world of make-believe. Also, the humorous, colourful illustrations include picture story sequences to stimulate the reader's own language and imagination.

A complete list of stories is given on the back cover and suggestions for using each book are made on the back pages.

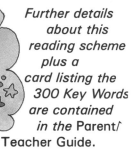

Further details about this reading scheme plus a card listing the 300 Key Words are contained in the Parent/ Teacher Guide.

This book belongs to

_____

_____

British Library Cataloguing in Publication Data
Murray, W. (William) *(date)*
    The dream.
    1. English language—Readers
    I. Title   II. Corby, Jill   III. Trotter, Stuart   IV. Series
    428.6
    ISBN 0-7214-1319-6

First edition

Published by Ladybird Books Ltd Loughborough Leicestershire UK
Ladybird Books Inc Auburn Maine 04210 USA

Printed in England

READ with me!

The dream

by WILLIAM MURRAY
stories by JILL CORBY
illustrated by STUART TROTTER

Ladybird Books

Tom and Kate are here.
Kate has a lunch box.
Tom has a lunch box.

Sam has a toy.
Sam likes the toy.
Kate and Tom have hats.

1

Tom and Kate go to school. They are with Mother. Tom has Kate's lunch box. Mother has Kate's hat.

2

3

Kate and Sam are in the trees.
They have fun.

4

Kate and Tom go into school.
Mother comes into school.

Sam can't come in. He must wait for Mother.

Mother says, Sam, you must wait here. You can't go with Tom and Kate.

1

Kate likes school. She likes to
have fun. Tom likes school.
He likes to read books.

2

3

Tom says, I like this, Kate.
You must read this book.
She looks and reads with Tom.

She says, I like to read books.

4

They like it at school.

Tom has a go. Look at me, he tells Kate. Come up with me. Up here, Kate.

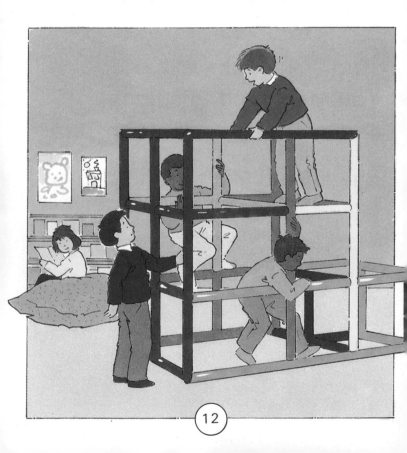

You must come up, he
tells her.

Wait, Tom, wait. Wait for me,
she says. I want to have a go.

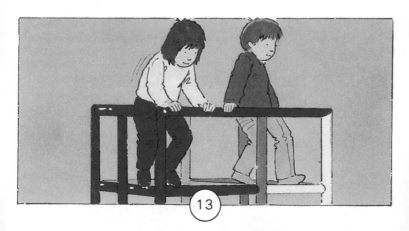

Kate, you have spots, Tom tells her. Come and tell the teacher.

Just look at me, she says.
Just look at the spots.
They look at the spots.

Look at me, says Kate to
her mother. I have spots,
she says. Just look at the spots.

Come home, Kate, says Mother.
You must come home with me.
You have spots and you can't
stay at school. Here is your
lunch box. Here is your hat.

Yes, I must go home, Kate
tells her mother. I can't stay at
school. Just look at the spots.

Mother and Kate are at home.
Mother has put Kate to bed.
She has to stay in bed.
Mother says, Have this, Kate.

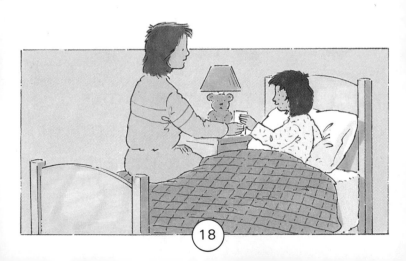

Sam has the toy. Sam wants Kate to have the toy. He puts it up on the bed.

Sam has put the toy on
Kate's bed.

You have spots, Kate tells
the rabbit.

The rabbit hops and hops.
Wait for me, she says.
You must wait for me, Rabbit.

On and on
they go.
They go fast.
Up and up.

Look, Kate tells the rabbit.
Look down there, now.
They have spots.

Just look down there, Rabbit.
I have spots. You have spots,
and they have spots.

Put me down now, Rabbit,
she says. I want to stay there.

Hop, hop, now.
On we go, Rabbit.

On they go. They go fast over the water.
Rabbit, see the fish down there.

See the fish in the water.
They have spots just like me.

On we go now, over the water.

You must not put me
down there, she says. I can't
stay there.

You must go on, Rabbit, over
the trees. Look at that down
there. Can you see that?
Just look at the spots.

They all have spots. They look up at you and me. We all have spots.

Put me down over there, please, Rabbit.

Hop, please hop, Kate tells the rabbit. See the sand over there. Look at all the sand.

That has spots like me,
she says. We can't stay here.
Please go on, Rabbit.

Look, there are lots of rabbits
down there. See all the rabbits
with spots. Lots and lots
of spots.

Go down now, Rabbit, please
go down. Please put me down
with the rabbits. I like it here,
she says.

I want to play with the
rabbits. I do like that rabbit
with lots of spots. And that
rabbit likes me.

We can play on the sand,
says Kate. I do want to play
with all the rabbits. Please can
we stay here?

We all like to play on the sand.
We go round and round
on the sand.

We all go round and round.
We go fast. We all go round
faster and faster and faster.

Kate stays at home.
Her mother looks for her spots.
You have no spots now,
she tells her. No spots at all.

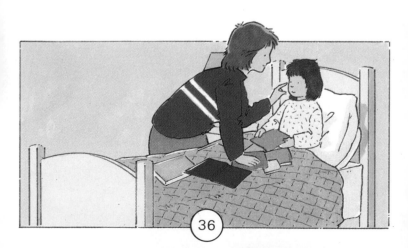

Kate says, Please can I go
to school now?
Yes, you can go now, says
her mother. Here is your
lunch box. Come to school
with Tom.

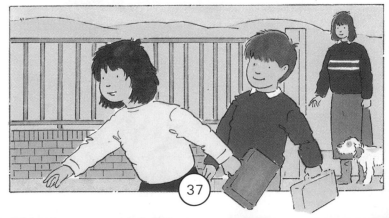

They are at school.
Kate reads her book.
I do like your book, Kate,
says Tom.

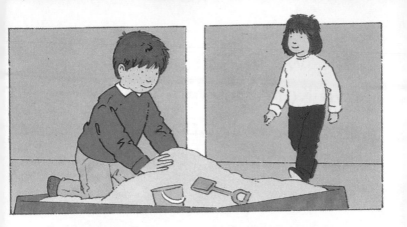

Tom plays with the sand.
Can I do that? says Kate.
Tom, she says, I can see
lots of spots on you.

You have spots now.

Tom, we must tell the teacher, says Kate. And you must go home to bed. Come and tell the teacher.

She can tell Mother to come
to school. Here is your lunch box.
Tom has to go home
with Mother.

Words introduced in this book

Number of words used............................38
The Key Words are the same as those introduced in Book 5.

Counting

How many fish?

How many rabbits?

How many cows?

Notes for using this book

The words, pictures and planning of this book are designed to:

✱ *help the child to learn to read*

✱ *help you to make learning an exciting and enjoyable experience for her**

✱ *encourage lots of conversation*

✱ *help her to become confident in her own ability*

✱ *encourage her powers of observation, understanding and sense of humour.*

When your child is ready and keen to learn to read (a Reading Readiness checklist is given in the Parent/Teacher Guide*) introduce this book just like any other picture storybook. Find a quiet, comfortable place and either read the book all the way through or read and talk about one page at a time. Point to the words and show that reading goes from left to right.*